Krustnkrum!

Distributed to Schools and libraries
in the United States by
ENCYCLOPAEDIA BRITANNICA EDUCATIONAL CORP
310 South Michigan Ave.
Chicago, Illinois 60604

ISBN 089565-744-9
Library of Congress Cataloging-in-Publication Data
available upon request

Krustnkrum!

author: Anne-Marie Chapouton
illustrator: Vincent Penot

The Child's World
Mankato, Minnesota

"Huh? What? You mean…?

Who, me?

Go to the bakery

and get the bread
all by myself?"
How awful!!!

Suppose a witch grabbed

me by the pantsleg

and tied me up

like a salami

and shut me in a cellar

with RATS in it?!!

And what if the street turned

into a dark forest

with wolves in the undergrowth

and poisonous plants

with creeping vines

twined around my feet

for two hundred years —

or a thousand years, even?

And a dragon

might come along, too.

Belching clouds of smoke

through his nose.

And I could be
turned into a frog —
Forever!

Aah! There's the bakery!
Good thing it isn't a
witch house, after all.

It's nice and warm
and it smells good.

"Good morning, ma'am!

One loaf of french bread, please.

Thank you very much.

Good-bye!"

Right! That takes care of that!
This loaf is also a
magic wand, and it'll
keep me safe and sound.

ZAP with the magic wand.

Krustnkrum!

I can turn

all the witches around here
into cats and dogs.

ZAP with the magic wand.

Krustnkrum!

The forest trees

and the vines

turn into lamp posts

and red 'stop' lights

and green 'go' lights.

And the wolves
are big black
garbage cans now

and can never,

never, never

lift a paw again.

ZAP with my magic wand.

Krustnkrum!

That's the big dragon

turned into a big truck

belching smoke

from the back.

Thanks, magic wand.

Krustnkrum!

I'm home again.

I'm safe again.

"Here you are, Mom! Here's the bread!
— Huh? The change?
Oh, boy! I forgot
to pick it up from the counter!"

ZAP with my magic wand.
Krustnkrum!

Look out, all of you!
I'm on my way again.

THE CHILD'S WORLD LIBRARY

THE LOVE AFFAIR OF MR. DING AND MRS. DONG

LULU AND THE ARTIST

THE MAGIC SHOES

THE NEXT BALCONY DOWN

OLD MR. BENNET'S CARROTS

THE RANGER SMOKES TOO MUCH

RIVER AT RISK

SCATTERBRAIN SAM

THE TALE OF THE KITE

TIM TIDIES UP

TOMORROW WILL BE A NICE DAY

THE TREE POACHERS